The Shade Tree

Suzy Lee

Translated by Helen Mixter

ALDANA LIBROS

 GREYSTONE KIDS

VANCOUVER / BERKELEY / LONDON

Once upon a time, in a village, there was a huge, old tree.

As the sun moved across the sky, the tree's shade grew and shrank, then grew again.

A young traveler had seen the tree in the distance.

He saw that the people of the village liked to lie in its shade to rest and cool down.

He decided to come and join the villagers.

But suddenly there was a shout.

"Everyone leave right now! How dare you sit here? This shade belongs to me!"

The traveler turned to a man who looked very rich and asked, "Are you saying that the shade has an owner? And that it is yours?"

"Of course!" said the rich man. "This tree is on my land. Isn't it surrounded by my fields? This tree was planted by my father's father's father so it is MY tree. And the shade is cast by MY tree, so it belongs to me!"

And he lay down in the shade.

The traveler said, "Oh. I guess you are right. So, if you own the shade, maybe you could sell it to me so I can sit here as long as I want."

The rich man thought the traveler was very foolish. But he saw a chance to make some money.

"Of course," he said.

The traveler emptied his pockets of all the money he had, and the rich man grinned and accepted it. "You've bought the shade and now it's yours. There's no denying it."

The traveler replied, "I've paid
you for this shade. Now it's mine
and you can't ever deny it."

The rich man went home with a big smile on his face.

The traveler invited the villagers to come and rest. "Now that the shade is mine, you can lie here whenever you want," he said.

And the villagers thanked him and happily relaxed.

By now the sun had begun to set and
the villagers went home, one by one.

Only the traveler stayed alone in
the tree's lengthening shade.

As the shade grew longer
the traveler moved with it—

Suddenly a furious scream broke the
silence. "Get out! How dare you?
Who said you could come in here?"

The traveler replied calmly, "Didn't you sell the tree's shade to me? Isn't it, therefore, mine wherever it falls? There's no denying it."

From then on, the traveler went in and out of the rich man's house whenever the shade was covering it. He rolled, and ran, and danced and tumbled and lay down.

Eventually the rich man muttered, "There's no denying it," and abandoning the house, moved away from the tree and its shade.

The traveler decided to settle down
and live in the rich man's house.
Why not? He owned it much of the time.
It is said that he lived a long and happy
life there.

And the huge, old tree grew bigger
and bigger. Everyone in the village
enjoyed great happiness in its shade.

First published in English by Greystone Books in 2023
Originally published in Korea in 2021 as 그늘을 산 총각.
Published by arrangement with BIR Publishing Co., Ltd.
Text and illustrations copyright © 2021 by Suzy Lee
English translation copyright © 2023 by Helen Mixter

23 24 25 26 27   5 4 3 2 1

Aldana Libros / Greystone Books Ltd.
greystonebooks.com

Cataloguing data available from Library and Archives Canada
ISBN 978-1-77840-018-6 (cloth)
ISBN 978-1-77840-019-3 (epub)

English jacket and text design by Jessica Sullivan

Printed and bound in China on FSC® certified paper at
Shenzhen Reliance Printing. The FSC® label means that materials
used for the product have been responsibly sourced.

Greystone Books thanks the Canada Council for the Arts, the British Columbia
Arts Council, the Province of British Columbia through the Book Publishing Tax
Credit, and the Government of Canada for supporting our publishing activities.

Canadä

Greystone Books gratefully acknowledges the xʷməθkʷəy̓əm (Musqueam),
Sḵwx̱wú7mesh (Squamish), and səlilwətaɬ (Tsleil-Waututh) peoples on
whose land our Vancouver head office is located.